Hercules the Hero

A myth from Ancient Greece

Michaela Morgan

Illustrated by
Glen McBeth

CONTENTS

OXFORD
UNIVERSITY PRESS

Dear Reader,

The stories of Hercules have been told for thousands and thousands of years.

They have been passed from person to person to person ... and now to you.

In Ancient Greece, children will have heard the same story that you are going to read.

It is the story of the first ever Superhero.

Michaela Morgan

Enjoy the story!

Chapter 1

Gods and Heroes

Long, long ago in Greece, the gods lived high in the sky.

The ordinary little humans lived down on the ground. But in between gods and humans there was another race.

We call them ...

... the heroes.

Have a look at them.

Jason

Atlanta

Perseus

• *Perseus:* (say) 'pur-see-uss.'

Heroes were half god, half human. They were larger than life, stronger than strong, braver than brave. They were born to battle beasts and mangle monsters.

All the heroes had special powers. The biggest hero of them all was Hercules.

HERCULES
NO: 1
TOP HERO

• *Hercules:* (say) 'hurk-you-leez.'

5

When Hercules was just an itty bitty baby, an enemy sneaked along and put two snakes in his cot. These were deadly snakes with fierce fangs full of venom.

What did baby Hercules do?

He picked them up, one in each hand and ...

... rattled them.

Ga ga gaaaa rattle snakes!

This lad will go far!

As the years went by, Hercules grew stronger ...

and **stronger** ...

and **stronger**.

But Hercules was half human and he had a lot to learn.

The gods looked down and spoke about him.

He needs tests!

He needs quests!

A good job will help him settle down!

Then the gods spoke to Hercules:

You have lessons to learn. You must go to work for King Eurystheus. If you do everything you are told you will pass our tests.

King Eurystheus was a nasty man ...

... and he hated Hercules.

He decided to give Hercules twelve impossible tasks.

The King smiled a false smile and turned to Hercules. 'Your first task is to kill the Giant Lion,' he said.

No one could kill the Giant Lion. It had a very special skin. Arrows just bounced off it. Knives just buckled.

Other hunters had tried to fight the lion. They had never been seen again.

They had all been pounced on ... and eaten.

'Hee hee,' sniggered King Eurystheus. 'That's the end of Hercules the Hulk!'

TASK 1
KILL THE
GIANT LION

Chapter 2

Hercules and the Giant Lion

Hercules tracked the lion, took careful aim and fired his arrows.

Ping they went as they bounced off.

So Hercules threw stones.

Clunk they went as they bounced off.

He threw rocks.

He threw boulders.

He threw trees. KERRRRRASH!

Nothing worked.

Luckily, Hercules could run like the wind!

Then Hercules tried using his brain.

Hercules was clever. He waited until nightfall. Then he sneaked into the entrance of the lion's cave and he blocked the exit.

The lion could not run now and had no room to pounce. All he could do was wrestle. And Hercules was a star wrestler.

ROUND
1
DING DING!

'Haroooo!' cried Hercules and he wrestled the lion to the ground.

Using only his mighty hands, Hercules overpowerd the Giant Lion.

His hands are lethal weapons.

Hercules took the lion's skin and wore it as a cloak. He wore the lion's gaping jaws as a helmet.

This is what he looked like.

Now Hercules was a superhero with a super costume that no arrows, knives – or teeth could get through to harm him. Result!

When King Eurystheus saw Hercules clad in the lion's skin thundering back down the road, he was terrified.

The quivering King ran and hid in a big storage jar. From inside this jar King Eurystheus gave his next order.

Your next task is to destroy the Hydra!

Chapter 3

Hercules and the Hydra

The Hydra was a beast with many heads – and one idea. Its one idea was to destroy everything in its path. Many had tried to fight it. All had failed.

Imagine this awful beast rising before you, rearing its many heads. All the heads have razor teeth, blazing eyes ... and the foulest breath.

The Hydra's breath was so foul it was lethal. One whiff – and you were dead.

And its feet! They were even worse! Even smelling the *footprints* of this foul beast would kill an ordinary man.

Luckily, Hercules was no ordinary man. He set off and took his young nephew Iolaus with him.

Bravely they made their way into the swamp where the creature lurked. The stench was vile.

Hercules drew his sword and the fight began.

• *Iolaus:* (say) 'aye-oh-lay-us.'

With a swish of his sword Hercules cut off one of the Hydra's heads. But before he had time to cheer and say 'Yesssssss!' two more heads had grown back in its place!

Swish, Swish. Hercules chopped off two more heads. Immediately, four more heads grew back.

Hercules was good at sums. He worked out that he couldn't win like this.

Just when Hercules had decided it couldn't get any worse … it got worse.

A giant crab grabbed hold of the hero's leg.

Iolaus was a quick thinker. He swung his burning torch to frighten off the crab.

Then each time Hercules chopped off a Hydra head, Iolaus seared the wounded stump. With a sizzle he stopped another head from growing.

The Hydra was defeated.

'I couldn't have done it without you boy,' said Hercules as they set off back to King Eurystheus.

The second task was done.

Chapter 4

The Deer with Golden Antlers

King Eurystheus was so scared of Hercules now that he stayed in his jar.

His voice echoed inside it.

Bring me the deer that belongs to the goddess Diana!

Now this deer was very special. It was a favourite of the hunting goddess. Its antlers were made of pure gold. It was fleet of foot ... and it was very hard to find.

For one whole year Hercules hunted the deer. Finally, one day he caught a glimpse of it. He did not want to kill or harm the deer.

So he took VERY careful aim and just pinned it down without drawing blood.

Proudly, Hercules led the golden animal back to King Eurystheus.

Chapter 5

The Wild Boar

Was the King pleased?

He was not.

He immediately sent Hercules off to find another fierce creature – a giant wild boar. But in next to no time, Hercules came stomping back with the wild boar carelessly slung over his shoulders.

King Eurystheus was filled with anger. This time he thought up a truly terrible task.

Chapter 6

A Stinky Job

'You must clean the stables of King Augeas.
said the King.

Now *you* may have to tidy your room
sometimes. That might seem like hard work –
but this was MUCH worse.

You'd better hold your nose!

King Augeas had a massive stable and in
it he kept a huge number of animals. He had
hundreds upon hundreds of horses,
thousands and thousands of cows, millions
of chickens ...

... and sheep and goats.

He had kept animals for countless years and
he had NEVER, **EVER** cleaned up after them.
Vast heaps of dung had piled up over the years.
Hercules held his nose. And shook his head.
This was a real stinker of a job.

Did Hercules have an enormous bucket
and a gigantic spade?

He did not.

But he did have heroic strength. He also
had imagination. So this is what he did ...

He rolled up part of the earth and joined
two rivers together and washed the stables
clean! He didn't even get his hands dirty!

Was that enough for King Eurystheus? No! He wanted more.

He asked Hercules to hunt down some birds. These were not little fluffy tweety birds. Oh no! These birds had beaks of bronze and claws of copper – and jaws that could crush a man. And that's what they did. They swarmed in the swamps and they feasted on flesh.

Plus their droppings were DEADLY!

Chapter 7

The Man-Eating Birds

Hercules took his nephew along for the adventure. Together they tracked these cruel birds down to their swamp. But every time Hercules put a foot on the swampy ground the ground tried to swallow him up. The birds hid in the trees safely out of reach.

Slurp!

'We could shoot them easily if they would take off and fly,' muttered Iolaus – and that's when he had a brilliant idea.

Iolaus played loud music. He danced a crazy dance. He stamped and stomped and whooped. The birds took flight. Then the hero and his nephew loosed their arrows. Job done!

Chapter 8

The Burping Bull and the Hungry Horses

For his next adventure, Hercules had to catch the Cretan bull. Catching a bull is bad enough but this was a burping bull – and he belched flames.

Hercules wrestled the bull to the ground. The lion skin protected Hercules from the flames.

Hercules wins!

King Eurystheus immediately sent Hercules off again. This time the task was to capture the Mares of Diomedes.

'What are they?' asked Hercules.

'Horses,' the King replied.

'With many heads?' asked Hercules.

'No,' said Eurystheus.

'Do they belch flames?'

'No'

'Do they have razor claws?'

'No'

'Easy peasy!' thought Hercules and off he went.

King Diomedes welcomed him.

That's when Hercules found out what those horses ate ...

The Mares of Diomedes dined on flesh.

Hercules fought with the King. In the end it was Diomedes that became the dinner.

Diomedes was such a bitter, tough, old king that the mares lost their taste for flesh. They became vegetarians and became quite calm. Hercules led them back to King Eurystheus.

Chapter 9

The Amazon Queen

For his ninth task, Hercules was sent to
the land of the Amazons to get a belt from
a queen.

But this was no ordinary belt. This was no
ordinary queen.

Hippolyte was Queen of the Amazons.

The Amazons were all women and all
skilled warriors. They were archers and
fine fighters.

Hippolyte listened to Hercules and agreed to give him the belt.

It was all going so well ... and then an enemy started a rumour.

'Hercules is going to kidnap the Queen ...'

Fierce fighting broke out and Hercules escaped by a whisker!

Chapter 10

The Monster's Dog

It wasn't long before King Eurystheus sent Hercules off to find something else. This time the King wanted cattle. But of course these were no ordinary cows. They belonged to Geryon.

Geryon was a monster with three heads and three sets of legs. He also had a fierce dog, which guarded the cattle. This dog only had two heads but each head had a set of razor teeth.

The dog leapt at Hercules. His razor teeth gleamed in the sun. Drools of saliva slobbered from his hungry mouth.

But Hercules had no fear of such creatures now. With a biff of his club Hercules sorted that guard doggy out. Then he rounded the cattle up and off he went.

Chapter 11

The Weight of the World

For his eleventh test, Hercules was sent to get an apple.

Of course, he wasn't just sent to get an apple from the local supermarket. Oh no, these apples were grown in a magical grove, protected by magical girls – and a dragon. But help was at hand.

'I can get those apples for you,' boomed a voice. 'My name is Atlas. I hear you are a strong man, Hercules.'

'I am the strongest man on earth!' Hercules boasted.

'Then you can hold my burden,' said Atlas. 'Just hold it for a minute while I get the apples.'

Hercules agreed.

Ooof! What a weight was put on his shoulders! It was the weight of the world.

The gods had given Atlas the task of holding up the world.

Atlas thundered off and soon he was back with the apples.

'I feel so light without all that weight!' grinned Atlas. 'And you are doing such a super job. I'll see you later. Cheerio!'

'But that's not our deal!' Hercules complained. 'That's not fair!'

Atlas didn't care. He was too busy stretching and skipping and leaping and twirling.

'I feel as light as air!' he sang.

Hercules knew that he was not as big and strong as Atlas – but he was *clever*.

'Before you skip off,' said Hercules, 'can you get me a pillow for my shoulder?'

'All right,' said Atlas. 'You can use the one I had.'

'Will you just lift the world up and pop the pillow on my shoulders?' asked Hercules.

Atlas took the weight of the world and in that split second Hercules slipped out and left the world back on Atlas' shoulders.

'Sorry!' said Hercules. 'But we all have our tasks and *that* job was given to you.'

Chapter 12

The Hound
of Hell

For the last task, King Eurystheus sent
Hercules to the Land of the Dead, to battle
with the Hound of Hell.

*That's the last we'll see
of him! **No one** comes
back from there!*

Hercules travelled to the ends of the earth
... and beyond.

Finally he came to Hades, the hellish Land
of the Dead. It lay beyond a wide and chilly
river – the River Styx. It was too wide and
deep for Hercules to cross. But there was
a boat and a boatman.

'Will you ferry me across, please?'
Hercules asked.

The boatman turned to face him. He wore a grey hooded robe. His face was invisible but his voice croaked, 'No! Not Unless you pay me with your life.'

Hercules had travelled far and learned much. He would not be stopped now. He glowered so fiercely that the bully boatman gave in. Then slowly, slowly the boatman ferried Hercules across to the Land of the Dead.

It was dark. Very dark. And yet at the same time there were shadows. Grey shadows writhed and whirled in the air. And there were sounds. Shrill screams. Distant howls. And a sort of hissing.

Hercules peered through the gloom …

... three pairs of evil yellow eyes glowered back at him. It was Cerberus, the three-headed Hound of Hell.

On each head there were swarms of lashing serpents. In each mouth, there were rows of teeth, glinting like knives.

GRRRRRRRRRRRROWLLLLLLLL!

Cerberus pounced.

But Hercules was wearing the lion skin.
The serpents could not sting through it.
The deadly teeth could not rip through it.

Hercules wrestled the hound to the ground. He used all the force of his mighty hands.

He used everything he had learned in his other adventures,

until ...

... Cerberus, the Hound of Hell submitted.

Hercules had achieved the impossible.
He had fought the Hound of Hell.
He returned from the Land of
the Dead.
The gods smiled on him.

From then on, Hercules lived a long and happy life.

At the end of his days he died a peaceful death. He had earned his place in the Heavens so the gods gave him an honoured place with them on Mount Olympus.

Hercules became a god.

GOD!